THE STORY OF KITES

BY

Ying Chang Compestine

ILLUSTRATED BY

YongSheng Xuan

Holiday House / New York

Long ago in China, children helped their parents in the rice fields. During the fall, they would chase birds away from the harvest.

One day Ting, Pan, and Kùai—the three Kang boys—were taking turns marching through their fields. They blew whistles and banged pots and pans to scare away the birds.

Tweeeeee!

Bang!! Klang!!

"Why do the birds always eat our rice?" asked Ting.

"Because they're hungry like me!" Kùai sat down and picked up his noodle bowl. "If I could fly, I'd chase those birds away."

Pan stopped blowing his whistle. "Is it break time yet? I have to do my math homework."

Ting stopped banging. "My arm's tired. My lips are numb."

Just as Kùai was about to pick up his chopsticks, a big gust of wind blew past the boys. Ting's straw hat and Pan's homework flew into the sky. Kùai's chopsticks rolled into the field. The boys ran after their belongings as fast as they could.

When they finally caught up with their things, Kùai said, "If we had wings, we could fly."

"Wings?" Pan asked. "How do we get wings?"

"We can make them with straw," said Ting. "Did you see how high my hat flew?"

"My homework stayed up longer," Pan bragged. "Paper is lighter."

"I have a better idea," said Kùai. "I'm going to use feathers."

"Well, let's make wings," said Ting. "Then we can chase those birds in the sky."

It took months for the boys to make their wings. On a warm and windy spring afternoon, Ting, Pan, and Kùai climbed the steep hill near their village. Each boy wore a set of wings attached to his arms.

Ting's wings were made of woven straw. Pan's wings were made of paper and bamboo chopsticks. Kùai had the biggest wings, which were made of chicken feathers.

"Let's fly and chase away the birds in our fields," shouted Ting.

"Ready . . . set . . . FLY!" yelled Kùai.

The boys jumped.

They flapped their wings.

But they all went in one direction —

down.

Kersplash!

Kerplop!

Kersploosh!

They landed right in the middle of the rice field.

"What's happening?" cried a farmer. "Are rocks falling off the hill?"

"Did a chicken just fall from the sky?"

"Did a straw hat make that noise?"

All the villagers gathered around.

When Ting, Pan, and Kùai finally got out of the rice field, even their parents didn't recognize them.

"Oh, my wings," groaned Kùai.

"I told you chicken feathers wouldn't work," said Ting. "Chickens can't fly." He dragged his straw wings out of the mud.

"Let's try again, with real bird feathers," suggested Pan. His paper-and-chopstick wings stuck out of the mud.

All the villagers started to laugh and laugh and laugh. Even Mama and Papa Kang.

After the boys' baths, Kùai asked, "How are we going to get enough feathers to make new wings?"

"I'm not sure I want to try again," said Ting. "My mouth tastes like mud. My whole body hurts."

"Me too," said Pan. "And I didn't like it when everyone laughed at us."

"Maybe we're too heavy to fly," said Kùai. "I have another idea."

The next day, after school, the three boys painted scary faces on their straw hats. Soon a strong wind came up. As it swept through, their hats flew up into the sky, right into the middle of a flock of birds. The scary faces sent the birds fleeing. Jumping up and down, the boys cheered for their flying hats.

When the wind died down, the hats were nowhere to be found. But Pan's homework was still flying, and Kùai's chopsticks had rolled into the field again.

That night, Mama didn't let the boys have any Sweet Eight Treasures rice pudding, because they'd lost the hats, homework, and chopsticks. After dinner, they had to help Papa make new straw hats.

"We can't fly our hats anymore. It's too much work if we lose them again," Ting said.

"We're going to be in trouble with the teacher if we lose our homework again," said Pan. "But I love losing my homework, especially math." He grinned.

"I like losing my chopsticks. Then I don't have to wash them." Kùai giggled. "I know! Why don't we tie our chopsticks to the homework? Then we could tie a string to the chopsticks so they can't get away."

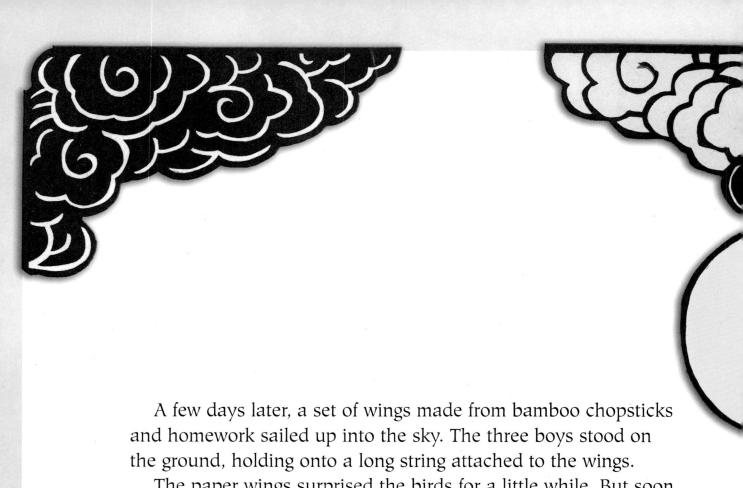

A few days later, a set of wings made from bamboo chopsticks and homework sailed up into the sky. The three boys stood on the ground, holding onto a long string attached to the wings.

The paper wings surprised the birds for a little while. But soon they grew used to the wings and ignored them.

"Boys!" yelled Mama. "Look at the birds. They are eating our rice. Go back to blowing and banging."

"It's not working. We need to make our wings scarier." Kùai picked up a pot and started banging.

"I know what we can do!" Pan picked up a whistle.

"Me too! I have an idea," said Ting.

"Let's see who can scare the most birds away," said Kùai.

Two weeks later, the boys returned to the hill above the rice fields. Each of them held something big in his hands.

"Look, the Kang boys are going to fly again," one villager yelled.

"You mean jump into the rice fields?" said another.

"Oh dear, they are wearing their nice clothes," Mama said. "Papa, quick, go stop..."

Before Mama could finish her sentence, the three boys let go of what was in their hands.

Ting launched a colorful phoenix with a long tail. Pan released a blue butterfly. Kùai tossed a big dark bird into the sky. As the gentle breeze blew, the tail of the phoenix danced around and the butterfly's wings flapped up and down.

All the villagers gathered around.

"What are those?"

"Where is that music coming from?"

"Is it coming from the dark bird?"

"Yes, there's a bamboo flute tied underneath it."

"Listen! The wind is playing the flute!"

"Look! The birds all flew away!"

Mama and Papa ran up the hill, and all the villagers followed.

When they found the Kang boys, they were surprised at what they saw. Each boy had tied his invention to a big tree. They were sitting under the trees eating Long-Life Noodles.

"What are those things doing in the sky?" asked one of the villagers.

Ting put down his bowl. "They are there to scare away the birds, so we don't have to blow whistles or bang pots and pans anymore."

"What are they called?" asked another villager.

Ting and Pan looked at Kùai.

Kùai said, "Since they make music like the strings of the *zheng* as they fly on the wind, I call them *fengzheng*—wind *zheng*—kites."

"Can you teach us how to make them?" asked another villager.

The boys nodded.

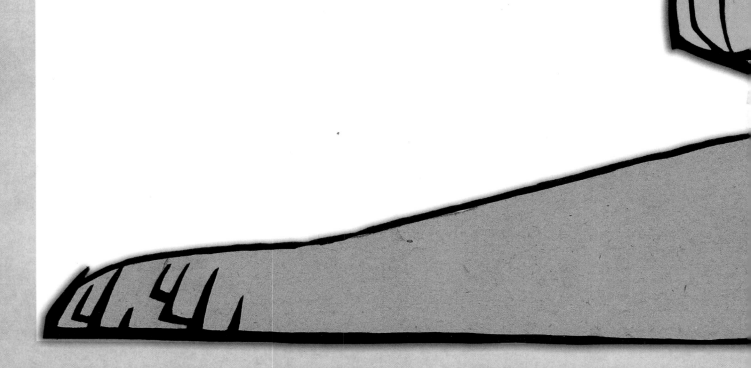

The Kang family opened the very first kite factory in China. They made kites of all colors and shapes. And best of all, no more birds came to eat their village's rice, because the sky was full of kites—dragons, fish, flying tigers, and phoenixes.

AUTHOR'S NOTE

Kites originated in China. An ancient Chinese philosopher, Mo Di, flew a kite twenty-four hundred years ago, which may have been one of the first in the world. Later, the kite spread to other Asian countries and from there around the globe.

There is no exact record of how or why the kite was invented. A common theory suggests that it was inspired either by the sight of the wind blowing a straw hat or by flying birds. Because the Chinese believed the soul was like a flying bird, the kite was especially symbolic. A flying kite would scare any evil out of the sky and protect the soul.

Today in China, people celebrate festivals with kites. During the spring Festival of the Lantern and the fall Festival of Climbing Heights, kites are flown throughout the country, generally from high ground.

There are many varieties of kites. Some carry small candle lanterns, while others carry fireworks that are timed to explode high in the sky. Among the most impressive kites are musical ones. One type of kite dangles mussel shells that make a rattling sound in the wind, while another type has a drum and a cymbal at the top. Still other kites carry bamboo flutes that sound like harps in the wind. Strips of rawhide are stretched taut on the frames of other kites, and sometimes bamboo bows are also attached.

The wind plays these kites like a musician playing a never-ending lullaby on a *zheng*, a Chinese stringed instrument. This led to the Chinese name *fengzheng* meaning "wind *zheng*," as the Kang boys call their invention.

Homemade Diamond Kite

With the help of an adult, you can make your own kite by following the steps below.

You will need:

Two long sticks or homemade chopsticks. Have an adult help you cut the sticks, so that one stick is about two-thirds the length of the other, 12 and 18 inches, for example.

A small knife

A roll of string

Scissors

Glue or softly cooked rice. The Kang boys used rice paste to glue their kites together.

A big piece of paper—try using newspaper, white paper, or even your old math homework!

A marker

1. Center the short stick one-third of the way down the longer stick to make a cross.
2. Secure the two sticks together by tying a piece of string around the joints three times, crossing both ways. Tie it with a knot. A dab of glue will help secure the knot.
3. Have an adult notch the ends of each stick with the knife.

4. Starting at the bottom of the longer stick and moving clockwise, slot a piece of string into all four notches, pulling the string tight all the way around to make a diamond shape. The string ends should meet at the bottom of the longer stick. Secure the string there with a double knot. You can trim off the remaining string or leave a length for the tail.

5. Lay the frame over your homework or other paper. Mark around the edges where you will cut the paper, leaving a 1-inch margin outside the string frame, and trimming the corners so that the sticks won't be covered.

6. After cutting out the paper, spread glue all around the edges where the frame will rest. Press the frame gently onto the paper. Fold the edges of the paper over the string of the frame.

7. To make the bridle, which is the loop of string on a kite that attaches the frame to the line, first cut a piece of string that is the length of one short edge plus one long edge of the kite. Tie one end of the string around the top of the kite. Make a loop one-third of the way down the length of the kite and knot it. Tie the other end to the bottom of the kite. Trim off any leftover string.

8. To make the tail, use a length of string about five times the height of the kite. Take scraps of paper about 2 x 3 inches and tie them along the tail string. Attach the tail to the frame.

9. Tie one end of the ball of string to the loop in the bridle.

Now your kite is ready to fly! You can be creative like the Kang boys by drawing on the kite or decorating the tail.

Kite Safety

1. Don't fly a kite in a thunderstorm or in the rain.
2. Don't fly a kite near electric wires or trees.
3. Don't fly a kite on a busy street or a steep slope.
4. Don't run backwards when launching a kite.
5. Wear your running shoes.

How to Fly a Kite

1. Try to stand on high ground, such as a hill. Plan where you are going to run before launching your kite.

2. Standing with your back to the wind, hold the kite in the air. When the wind blows, let go of the kite. Turn and run as fast as you can into the wind. When you feel the wind tug at the kite, release some of the string. Let the wind do the job for you. Each time you feel a tug, let out more of your string. You will get better with practice.

To Vinson Ming Da, my precious kite flier;
to Greg, the wind beneath my kite
Y. C. C.

To my papercut and kites master, Guo Cheng Yi
Y. S. X.

Text copyright © 2003 by Ying Chang Compestine
Illustrations copyright © 2003 by YongSheng Xuan
All Rights Reserved
The illustrations were created with cut paper
in traditional Chinese style.
Printed in the United States of America
www.holidayhouse.com
First Edition

Library of Congress Cataloging-in-Publication Data

Compestine, Ying Chang.
The story of kites / by Ying Chang Compestine;
illustrated by YongSheng Xuan.—1st ed.
p. cm.
Summary: Long ago in China, three brothers become tired of chasing birds
from their family's rice fields and experiment with ways to make the job easier.

ISBN 0-8234-1715-8 (hardcover)

[1. Brothers—Fiction. 2. Farm life—China—Fiction.
3. Kites—Fiction. 4. China—History—Fiction.]
I. Xuan, YongSheng, ill. II. Title.
PZ7.C73615 Ste 2003
[Fic]—dc21
2002027375